Trixie
the Halloween
Fairy

To Susan, who always has a Halloween
trick (and treat!) up her sleeve

Special thanks
to Kristin Earhart

ORCHARD BOOKS
338 Euston Road, London NW1 3BH
Orchard Books Australia
Level 17/207 Kent Street, Sydney, NSW 2000
A Paperback Original

First published in 2009 by Scholastic Inc.
First published in the UK in 2010 by Orchard Books.

HiT entertainment

A CIP catalogue record for this book is available
from the British Library.

ISBN 978 1 40831 138 7
7 9 10 8 6

Printed in Great Britain

The paper and board used in this paperback are natural recyclable
products made from wood grown in sustainable forests. The
manufacturing processes conform to the environmental regulations
of the country of origin.

Orchard Books is a division of Hachette Children's Books,
an Hachette UK company

Trixie
the Halloween Fairy

by Daisy Meadows

ORCHARD

www.rainbowmagic.co.uk

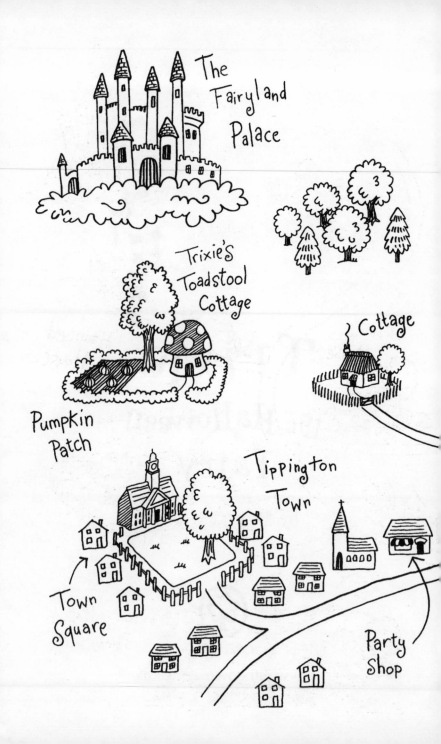

I, Jack Frost, have planned a nasty scare.
Indeed, all humans should beware.
Halloween will be all trick and no treat,
Since my goblins stole what makes the day so sweet.

To the world of humans the goblins go.
The magic sweets are lost and will stay so.
All kids in costume will have a mighty fright,
When they have no fun on Halloween night!

The
Chocolate
Chase

Contents

Buttons Barks

"I can't wait to show you the fairy wings," Rachel Walker said to her best friend, Kirsty Tate, as they climbed the stairs to Rachel's room.

"I'm looking forward to seeing them," Kirsty replied. "It will be so much fun to trick-or-treat together!"

Kirsty was visiting Rachel for the weekend, and it just happened to be Halloween! They were both going to dress up as fairies and go trick-or-treating in Tippington.

The two girls exchanged smiles as Rachel lifted the lid of a box. Inside were two sets of glittery fairy wings: one was pale pink and the other was light purple. There were also two fairy wands.

"Oh, Rachel! They look almost real," Kirsty said, giving her friend a secret smile. After all, the girls knew just how real fairies' wings looked, because they were friends with the fairies!

Rachel and Kirsty had first met when they were on holiday with their families on Rainspell Island. There, they had helped the Rainbow Fairies get back to Fairyland after they had been banished by wicked Jack Frost. Since then, the girls had had a lot more adventures, and the King and Queen of Fairyland always looked to them when Jack Frost was up to his old tricks.

"I'm going to try mine on," Kirsty said, carefully lifting up the pink pair of wings.

Just then, they heard a loud bark.
Buttons, Rachel's dog, raced into the
room. He bounded past Kirsty and
knocked over the box on his way to
the window.

"Buttons!" Rachel yelled as the
costumes flew up in the air. But Buttons
kept barking at something outside. Then
he turned to Rachel and whimpered.
"What is it, boy?" Rachel asked with
concern.

"Oh look! There's a kitten in the tree!"
Kirsty said, pointing out of the window.
The kitten was black from its nose to
its tail.

"That's
strange,"
Rachel said.
"Buttons
usually
likes cats."
Now
the big
sheepdog
pawed at
the window.
"Do you
think the kitten's
stuck?" Kirsty asked.
"Maybe it needs our help."

But at that moment, the little black cat leapt onto a nearby branch. It strutted past the window and seemed to look right at Buttons and the girls, then scurried down another tree.

Buttons let out a yelp, dashed from the room, and ran down the stairs.

"Strange," Rachel said with a laugh. Kirsty nodded before letting out a groan. "Oh no! Look at our costumes!" Rachel bent down and lifted up her wings.

The thin fabric had a big tear in it. Kirsty's wings looked the same.

"Buttons must have done this when he raced past," Rachel sighed.

"But that's not all that's wrong," Kirsty said, glancing around with a dismayed look on her face. "The glitter seems to have fallen off the fabric. The wings aren't shimmery any more. And one of our wands is missing!"

"I can't see my sparkly fairy tights, either," Rachel added, looking around the room and under her bed. She sat up and sighed.

"It looks like there could be something mysterious going on here," Kirsty said.

"Mysterious, or magical?" Rachel smiled.

Kirsty's eyes sparkled. She hoped her friend was right!

"Either way, I suppose we'll have to start all over again with our fairy costumes," she sighed.

"Let's go to the party shop to see what they've got," Rachel suggested. "We only have two days left until Halloween!"

Costume Chaos

Rachel and Kirsty made a list of what they needed to get from the party shop, and Rachel told her mum where they were going.

As they walked down the street, the girls wondered what had happened to the other parts of their costumes. "It doesn't make sense," Kirsty said. "I definitely remember seeing two wands in the box."

Rachel nodded in agreement. "I know, I did, too," she said. "But we'll find everything we need to make new costumes at the party shop. It's the best one in the area and I know the owner, Mrs Burns. She has lots of fantastic fairy costumes."

The girls walked towards the centre of town. The sun was out, and the air was cool and crisp.

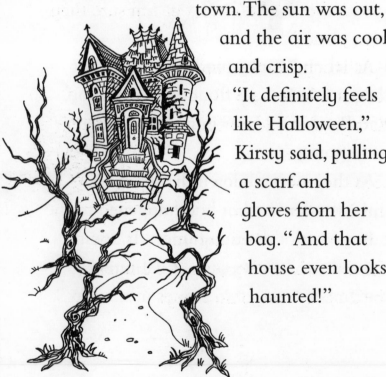

"It definitely feels like Halloween," Kirsty said, pulling a scarf and gloves from her bag. "And that house even looks haunted!"

Rachel knew exactly which house her friend meant. It was a three-storey Victorian mansion with a big porch and lots of windows. The house sat at the end of a long driveway that was lined with crooked trees. "Don't worry," Rachel assured Kirsty. "It's just an old house that nobody has lived in for years. There are stories that it's haunted, but I'm sure they aren't true."

As Rachel looked up, she let out a little gasp. "Look, Kirsty!" she exclaimed, sure that she had seen someone at the third-floor window.

But as she looked again, the figure had disappeared. Perhaps she'd been imagining things.

"What is it, Rachel?" asked Kirsty, looking puzzled.

"Oh, it was nothing. Never mind," said Rachel.

They continued on their way, chattering excitedly. Then, as they walked into the town square, the girls saw lots of other people heading for the party shop.

"It's always busy at this time of year," Rachel explained as she pushed open the door.

When they stepped inside, the girls gasped.

The shop was in total chaos. Parents and children stood everywhere, all looking upset. There was a long queue behind a sign that read 'Returns'.

Two grumpy mothers in the line were peering into their bags.

"My son's astronaut costume has bunny ears instead of an oxygen helmet," one complained, shaking her head.

"I bought a ballerina outfit, but it has fireman boots instead of ballet shoes," said the other.

"Both of them bought costumes that were mixed up?" Kirsty whispered in disbelief.

"Hmmn, something's definitely going on," Rachel replied. "Look, there's Mrs Burns," she said, pointing to a woman carrying a straw basket, but the shopkeeper didn't seem to notice the girls. She was too busy rushing around, clicking her tongue with concern as she looked at the jumbled shelves.

As the friends walked towards the back of the shop, all of the customers were grumbling. The girls passed a group of boys who were digging through a bin of hats and wigs, trying things on before noisily throwing them onto the floor.

No wonder the shop is in such a mess, Kirsty thought.

Just then, Rachel stopped. "This is where the fairy costunes are," she said, pointing to a nearby shelf, "but they're not here now."

"And what is here is all mixed up," Kirsty noted as she examined a parrot mask with a long grey trunk instead of a beak.

Next, she picked up a pretty princess hat. But instead of having ribbons flowing from the pointy top, there were rubber snakes with wagging red tongues.

"Yuck," Rachel declared.
"You can say that
again," a
twinkling
voice sang out.
With that,
a burst of
star-shaped
sparkles filled
the air, and a
tiny fairy flew
out from behind
the princess
hat. She was
wearing a short,
orange dress
with a silky black
sash, and black-and-
orange striped tights.

A star pendant hung around her neck, and she had a mischievous grin.

"You must be Rachel and Kirsty," the fairy said. "I'm Trixie the Halloween Fairy. I need your help!"

Three Treats

Rachel and Kirsty gasped in surprise. They couldn't take their eyes off the tiny fairy's glittery wings, which were especially sparkly in the dim shop.

"It's nice to meet you," Rachel and Kirsty said at once. They loved meeting new fairies!

"And it's a pleasure meeting you, too. You're quite famous in Fairyland," Trixie said, with a wink.

The girls smiled at each other. "Trixie, what's wrong?" Kirsty asked, her smile fading. "Why do you need our help?"

"Oh!" Trixie sighed. Her smile quickly fell into a frown. "Halloween is in terrible trouble."

"What's happened?" Rachel said.

Trixie sighed. "It all started yesterday," the fairy began. "I had just finished making my magic Halloween sweets. Every year I make three kinds of sweets: bars of chocolate, jellybeans and toffee apples." The fairy paused dreamily and licked her lips.

"Oh, where was I?" she said, blinking. "Ah, yes. I sprinkle one sweet from each batch with my special star-shaped fairy dust. These three enchanted sweets hold the Halloween magic! Without them, Halloween wouldn't be the same."

"What happened to the sweets?" Kirsty asked.

"They're missing!" Trixie cried. Kirsty and Rachel listened closely as Trixie told them that each sweet had an important job.

The bar of chocolate helped make sure everyone had a costume and looked special. The magic jellybean's job was to make sure there were plenty of sweets for everyone and that they tasted extra delicious. Finally, the toffee apple helped boost the Halloween spirit – it let everyone enjoy the magic of the day.

"I wrap the three magic sweets in special glittery orange wrappers," Trixie added, with a sigh.

"How lovely! I didn't even know you celebrated Halloween in Fairyland," Kirsty smiled.

"Oh yes," Trixie replied. "Halloween is one of the few days of the year when people in the human world believe in the magic that lives in Fairyland all the time. We all love it!" Then Trixie scowled. "Except Jack Frost. He doesn't want humans to have any fun. This year, he came up with a nasty plan."

Trixie explained that she was watering her pumpkin patch when she heard lots of noise.

"Oh no," Kirsty said, biting her lip.

"You've guessed it," said Trixie, crossing her arms.

The fairy's eyes were serious as she
told them that Jack Frost's goblins had
crept into her toadstool cottage to steal
the magic sweets. "They were almost at
the edge of Fairyland when I spotted
them: seven green goblins with chocolate
smeared on their hands and faces. Just as
I lifted my wand to stop them, Jack Frost
appeared. The icy magic from his wand

crashed into my star sparkles. His magic must have gone wrong because instead of taking the enchanted sweets, he hid them in the human world!"

"We have to get them back!" Rachel cried. She couldn't imagine Halloween without costumes, sweets and lots of fun.

"Thank you," Trixie said with a grateful smile. "But there's just one more thing." The fairy's deep brown eyes grew wide. "We can't let the magic sweets fall into the wrong hands. If someone who doesn't believe in Halloween eats one of them, the part of Halloween it looks after will be ruined forever."

Rachel and Kirsty gulped.

Just then, one of the noisy boys who had been rummaging through the hat bins stamped his feet. "It's not here!" he cried.

"I'm looking somewhere else." The other boys followed, all wearing a hat or a silly wig.

"Did you see that?" Kirsty asked.

"It's awful," Trixie said, shaking her head. "Those boys certainly don't have any Halloween spirit."

"And they didn't have any shoes,"

Rachel said with a smile. "But they did have big green feet."

"They did," Kirsty agreed. "Trixie, I think we've found some of the goblins!"

Goblins on the Go

Kirsty, Rachel and Trixie rushed after the goblins.

"I think they went in there," Rachel said, pointing to a heavy-looking door with a sign that read 'Store Room'.

"Then we have to go in there, too," Trixie announced. She pointed her wand, and the door opened with a burst of star sparkles.

"Trixie!" Kirsty whispered. "You have
to be more careful.

Someone might
see you!"

Trixie quickly
flew into
Kirsty's pocket
until they were
safely inside the
store room, which

was almost as big as the shop itself. There
were rows of shelves, each piled high with
boxes – but no sign of the goblins.

"Mrs Burns always has a basket of
sweets on the counter," Rachel whispered.
"Maybe she keeps a supply of them in
this store room."

"And maybe the bar of chocolate is
there, too!" Trixie exclaimed.

The girls had to tiptoe around open costume boxes that littered the floor.

"This room is as messy as the shop," Kirsty commented.

"It's because the magic bar of chocolate is missing," Trixie explained. "Everything that has do with costumes is all mixed up."

"That must be why our wings broke," Rachel said thoughtfully.

"And why the wand went missing," Kirsty added.

"Let's go and find those goblins and my sweets!" Trixie cried, and zoomed off.

The girls raced after the fairy, dodging piles of costumes as they went.

Just then, they saw blasts of icy sparks in the next aisle. Goblins! They slowed down and peeked around the corner.

"Jack Frost gave the goblins a wand," Trixie whispered. "You have to be careful. It can mix up anything."

A goblin with extra pointy ears was holding the wand. He aimed it at a tall goblin dressed as a policeman.

"I want to be the policeman!" he yelled,
but the goblin in the policeman costume
just shook his head. Icy bolts shot
from the other goblin's wand, and the
policeman's blue uniform
shirt changed to a
sparkly yellow top.

"Change it
back!" yelped
the tall goblin,
blowing on his
police whistle.

"No!" The
pointy-eared
goblin grinned,

then aimed the wand at
another goblin and turned his ferocious
dragon costume into a bright pink dress
with purple flowers.

"That explains the mismatched costumes," Kirsty whispered.

The other goblins were pulling down boxes and ripping through them.

"They must think one of the magic sweets is here," Trixie said.

At that moment, Kirsty saw a flash of something orange and glittery in one of the goblin's hands. "They've found something!" Kirsty cried, unable to control her excitement. "It must be the bar of chocolate. Let's get it!"

As soon as the goblins heard Kirsty, they stopped what they were doing and raced towards the back door.

Hot on the goblins' trail, the girls ran through the door and into the alley, with Trixie flying overhead. As they chased the goblins around the corner, they looked for another glimpse of the glittery wrapper. But the seven goblins were running too fast, dropping wigs and hats as they went.

"Oh no! They're heading for the town square," Rachel said, as the goblins made their way across the street to the grassy area in the centre of the village.

Trixie and the girls looked around frantically. They couldn't let anyone else spot the goblins! The three friends were gaining on the goblin gang, but they still had no idea which one had the magic sweet.

All at once, a black kitten sprung out of a tree and pounced down in front of the goblins.

"Yikes!" screeched the first goblin as he tripped and fell. When he tried to get up, another goblin toppled over him, then another, until they were all in a big heap.

"It's the little black cat we saw earlier," Rachel said happily. The kitten looked right at the girls and Trixie before bounding across the village green and out of sight.

"And here's the orange glittery thing we spotted earlier," said Kirsty, sounding disappointed. She picked up something from the ground. "It isn't a magic sweet wrapper at all." It was just an orange sparkly mask that a goblin had taken from the store room. "Now we have to start all over again."

"Don't worry, Trixie, we'll find the magic sweets," Rachel said, but when she looked around, she couldn't see Trixie anywhere.

Where had their fairy friend gone?

Lost and Found

The girls walked quickly away from the goblins, who were still in a big pile, and started searching for Trixie. But just then, the fairy zipped down from high in the sky.

"Have you found something?" Rachel asked hopefully.

"Not really," Trixie replied. "I was looking for Moonlight."

"Moonlight?" Kirsty said, shielding her eyes as she glanced up at the sunny sky.

"The little black kitten," Trixie explained with a small smile. "He must have got mixed up in the spells that sent the magic sweets into the human world."

"Is he your kitten?" Rachel asked.

"Not really, but he's been hanging

around my cottage in Fairyland ever since I started making my Halloween sweets," the fairy told them. "He's very brave, but he does tend to disappear suddenly!"

"We saw him this morning, too," Kirsty said. "At Rachel's house."

"I hope he doesn't get lost in the human world. I'm sure the king and queen would want me to take him back to Fairyland, but we have to find the magic sweets first," Trixie said.

Kirsty and Rachel knew they only had two days until Halloween, and they still needed to find all three magic sweets!

The three friends made their way back to the costume shop. Along the way, they picked up the costumes that the goblins had dropped in their mad dash from the store room.

"The magic bar of chocolate must still be at the shop," Kirsty said, picking up a discarded tiger mask.

"Or somewhere else," Rachel sighed. "I guess we'll just have to wait for the magic to come to us!" The Queen of Fairyland often gave the girls that same advice.

When they arrived back at the shop, Mrs Burns was trying to clean up the mess. "I just don't understand what happened," she was muttering to herself. "I don't like it when people are unhappy with their costumes. I can't even find the sweets that I usually give away. It doesn't feel like Halloween at all!"

Still, the shopkeeper smiled when she saw Kirsty and Rachel.

As soon as she heard that the girls
needed new fairy costumes, she hurried
off to find wings and other glittery items.

"Let's help tidy up," Rachel suggested.

Kirsty, Rachel and Trixie went to the
back of the shop and started to put things
back in the right place. When no one was
looking, Trixie used her wand to send
boxes of face paint and trick-or-treat
bags back to the shelves with a sparkle.
In no time at all, the floor was clear and
the shelves were almost full.

"If we don't find new wings, I could
always be a clown," Rachel said with a
laugh as she picked up a bright-red clown
wig. As she plopped it on her head, sweets
came showering down out of the wig and
landed in a heap on the floor.

"Look!" Kirsty exclaimed, pointing to

an orange glittery bar at the very top of the pile. "It's the magic bar of chocolate!"

"Oh!" Mrs Burns said, rushing forward. "You found our trick-or-treat sweets! Let's put them in the basket where they belong."

Kirsty held her breath as the shopkeeper bent down to gather the sweets. The girls kneeled down to help. Rachel gave Kirsty a worried glance as they watched Mrs Burns toss the orange glittery bar into the straw basket.

"It just hasn't felt like Halloween

without our basket of sweets," Mrs Burns
said, standing up and starting to walk
away. Kirsty's face dropped as she went
around the corner.

"What am I thinking?"
Mrs Burns asked
suddenly, hurrying back.
"Would you
like some sweets?"

As soon as Mrs
Burns made the
offer, Kirsty's hand
sprang forward to
grab the glittery
orange bar. "Thank you, Mrs Burns,"
she said, beaming. "It does feel more
like Halloween already." Kirsty held the
chocolate behind her back, and Trixie
quickly swooped down to pick it up.

"And look!" Mrs Burns exclaimed, pointing to something on the very top shelf. "I can see my favourite fairy wings. I wondered where they were hiding." The shopkeeper climbed up the old wooden ladder to pull the sparkly packages off the shelf. She handed one to Rachel and another to Kirsty. "You girls have been such a help. Please take these as a special thank you."

"Oh, Mrs Burns, they're beautiful," Rachel said with a delighted sigh.

"Thank you so much," added Kirsty.

As the girls grinned, they saw Trixie swoosh into the air behind Mrs Burns. The happy fairy turned the magic bar of chocolate to fairy-size and gave it a little kiss. Rachel and Kirsty watched her fly away, knowing she was heading straight back to Fairyland!

"Once Trixie returns the magic bar of chocolate to Fairyland, everyone's costumes will look fantastic," smiled Kirsty. "Now we just have two more magic sweets to track down, and we'll all have a very happy Halloween!"

The
Jellybean
Jaunt

Contents

All Dressed Up

"Happy Halloween!" Mr Walker said, snapping a picture of Rachel and Kirsty with his camera. "You look great!"

"Just like real fairies," Rachel's mum added, her hands clasped.

Rachel and Kirsty smiled at each other. They both wore beautiful, glittery wings on their backs. Kirsty was dressed in a short, purple, pleated skirt and a lilac cardigan with puffed sleeves.

Rachel had chosen a pretty green
jumper dress with ballet shoes. The girls'
lockets shimmered

around their
necks. The
lockets had
been gifts
from the
King and
Queen of
Fairyland.
"I wonder
where our newest
fairy friend could be,"
Kirsty whispered, suddenly concerned.
The best friends had not seen Trixie
since they had found the magic bar
of chocolate in the party shop the
day before.

Ding-dong! Ding-dong!

"I'll get that," Mr Walker offered. He put on a cowboy hat and headed to the front door. Rachel's mum followed him. She was wearing a matching cowboy hat with a long denim skirt. Her checked shirt was tied at the waist.

"We know that Trixie made it to Fairyland with the magic bar of chocolate," Rachel said under her breath. "All of our costumes look amazing! If the chocolate wasn't back in Fairyland, the costumes would still be mixed up."

"You're right. And I'm sure Trixie will turn up soon," Kirsty said with a sigh. It was almost time to go trick-or-treating, and they still had two more magic sweets to find!

Just then, Rachel's dad rushed into the living room. "Girls, do you know where our Halloween sweets went? They seem to have disappeared. Even the bowl has gone!"

Kirsty and Rachel looked at each other.

"We don't know where they've gone," Rachel replied. They didn't have any idea where the sweets were, but they did have an idea of why they were missing. It was

all because of Jack Frost and his pesky goblins!

"Well, there's a gang of ghosts at our door, and we don't have anything to give them!" Mr Walker rushed to the kitchen, his cowboy boots clip-clopping on the floor.

Buttons let out a bark.

"Buttons gets so nervous at Halloween," Rachel said, running towards the front door. She got there just in time to grab Button's collar. "It's OK, boy. He doesn't like the costumes," Rachel explained.

The girls opened the door and looked into the dusky night. The neighbourhood was starting to fill with firemen and superheroes, princesses and knights, dinosaurs and lions. They could see a large group of boys dressed as ghosts scampering down the street.

"Those ghosts didn't even wait for
Dad to find the sweets," said Rachel.

"And look! There's Moonlight. He's
running after the ghosts," Kirsty added
with a laugh.

The little black cat seemed intent
on catching up with the group.

Kirsty lowered her voice to a whisper.
"I wonder if those

ghosts are actually...
goblins?"

Just then, Rachel's
parents returned to
the front hall. Mr
Walker was rubbing
his chin. "I suppose

I'll have to get more sweets
at the local shop," he said. "It isn't
Halloween without something to give the
trick-or-treaters."

"You two should get going and have
fun," said Mrs Walker.

The two best friends grabbed their
bags and straightened their wings. Kirsty
waved as she headed out of the door.

"We'll see you at the party later,"

Rachel said, giving each of her parents
a quick hug.

"Yes, you girls are going to have a very
busy night!" Mr Walker replied.

Rachel and Kirsty gave each other
worried looks. Little did he know.
They still needed to find two more
magic sweets – and they were running
out of time!

All Trick, No Treat

As Kirsty and Rachel walked out onto the street, they saw some older boys.

"Hey! There's a stone in this sweet wrapper!" a boy in an alien costume shouted to his friends.

"Yuck! In mine, too!" a boy dressed as an American footballer spluttered, wiping his mouth on his sleeve. He threw the stone onto the ground. "That was a mean trick."

Rachel shook her head and sighed, watching the boys wander away. "I suppose we should trick-or-treat," she said, "and see what happens."

"Good idea," agreed Kirsty as they walked up the path to a house lit with lots of pumpkin lanterns placed on the steps. Golden lights flickered through their carved faces with a spooky glow.

"The Kemps live here," Rachel said.

"They're friends with my parents. They always have really yummy sweets."

"I hope they can find their sweet bowl," Kirsty said, raising her eyebrows.

"Trick or treat!" the girls sang out when the door opened.

A woman wearing a crown smiled at them. "Look at you!" Mrs Kemp said.

Then she paused and called over her shoulder. "Jack, come and see the fairies!"

A tall man with thick, white hair appeared behind Mrs Kemp.

"Are those real wings?" he teased. "You look like you could fly away." Then he held out a basket full of sweets for the girls.

Rachel and Kirsty looked at each other with surprise. The Kemps had sweets after all! There were mini chocolate bars, square fruit gums, jellybeans and lollipops.

"Thank you, Mr and Mrs Kemp," Rachel said, choosing a mini chocolate bar. Kirsty took a fruit gum.

"You're welcome," Mrs Kemp said, waving goodbye. "Happy Halloween!"

"You were right." Kirsty smiled as the girls walked down the path. "They had lots of yummy things! I love fruit gums."
Kirsty ripped open the paper wrapper and popped the red sweet into her mouth.

At once, her smile dropped and her nose scrunched up.

"Rachel," she said, "this doesn't taste very nice." She paused, moving the sweet around in her mouth. "It doesn't taste of anything at all."

Rachel, who had just taken a nibble of her chocolate bar, also frowned.

"You're right. They're *all* horrible!" said someone suddenly.

The girls immediately looked around, recognising the voice that echoed through the air. It was Trixie!

The tiny fairy fluttered into view with a cloud of star-shaped fairy dust trailing behind her. The dust sparkled against the dark night sky. "It's because the magic jellybean is still missing," Trixie explained.

"The jellybean not only makes sure there are plenty of sweets, but it also makes them yummy and delicious. We have to find it!"

"Oh, Trixie!" Kirsty cried. "We're so glad to see you!"

"And I'm glad to see you," Trixie replied. "But there's no time to chit-chat. I think I know where the magic jellybean might be!" With that, the little Halloween Fairy whizzed down the street.

A Sweet Clue

Rachel and Kirsty set off, running as fast as they could. They couldn't quite keep up with Trixie. The fairy was dodging trick-or-treaters as she zoomed ahead.

"Someone's going to see her if she's not careful," Rachel said, gasping for breath.

"And she's got to slow down," Kirsty puffed.

Just then, Trixie stopped in midair and looked back at the girls. "This is it!" she called, pointing to a cottage with a stone chimney and thatched roof. There was a single candle in the window, and Kirsty could just make out a broom propped up on the porch.

"Come on," Trixie said, grinning and zooming up to the door.

The cottage looked spooky in the moonlight, but the girls felt safe with Trixie nearby. They climbed up the creaky old porch stairs.

Trixie raised her wand, and a stream of fairy dust pushed the doorbell.

"Trixie, you have to hide!" Rachel insisted, holding open her bag. The fairy ducked inside just as the heavy wooden door swung open.

"Trick or treat!" the girls shouted.

A friendly face appeared around the edge of the door. The lady had straight black hair and wore a witch's costume. "Hello," she smiled. "Come and choose some sweets from my cauldron."

The girls peeked inside the tidy little cottage and saw a gigantic black pot right next to the door. It was empty.

"Oh no!" the lady exclaimed when she realised the sweets were gone. "You're only my second group of trick-or-treaters. I wonder if those rude little ghosts took them all." She bent over and swept her hand through the big iron pot, just to be sure that there was nothing inside. "Even the sweet with the pretty glittery orange wrapper is gone!"

Rachel and Kirsty exchanged glances.

"There were ghosts here before us?" Rachel asked.

"Yes, about six or seven of them. They just left," the lady said, taking off her tall, pointy hat and looking terribly sad. "This is the first Halloween I've had in this house," she added. "I wanted it to be fun."

Kirsty felt awful for her. "We know those ghosts," she said. "If they took your sweets, we'll get them back. Come on, Rachel." Kirsty gave the lady a small smile and a nod. Without another word, she marched down the porch stairs.

"We need to find the magic jellybean," Trixie said, fluttering out of Rachel's bag as soon as the girls were out of sight of the cottage. "If that lady is right, the ghosts must have it!"

"So all we have to do is find the ghosts – I mean, goblins," Kirsty replied. "And then all the Halloween sweets will be back where they belong."

"OK," Rachel agreed. "Where do we
start? It's getting dark, so it will be harder
to find them. And we don't even know
which way they went."

"First of all, I can make your wands
a little more useful," Trixie replied. The
fairy waved her own wand, and fairy dust
swirled around the wands in Kirsty's and
Rachel's hands. The wands began to glow

with a bright, silvery light. "And it would help if those wings really worked." With another twirl of Trixie's wand, the girls' wings began to sparkle. As the friends floated up into the air, they shrank down to fairy-size.

"That's much better, isn't it?" Trixie grinned, her hands on her hips. "Now, let's go and get those goblins!"

Playground Ghosts

The three fairy friends fluttered their wings until they were high above the trees. "We'll be able to spot that gaggle of ghosts much better from up here," Trixie said.

Kirsty and Rachel flew close behind Trixie. They held their wands in front of them to light the way. They were getting closer to the centre of town, and there were more people on the pavements and in the streets.

"Ooh, look!" Kirsty exclaimed. "I can see a group of ghosts down there." A streetlight cast a dim glow over the nearby playground. Rachel could just make out a cluster of ghosts hidden in the shadow of a tall tree.

"They have loads of sweets!" Trixie said. "The magic jellybean might be there."

The goblins' voices carried through the cool night air. They were grunting and grumbling as they ate lots of sweets and then threw the wrappers all around.

Kirsty gasped. "Oh no! They're eating all the sweets!" she cried. She remembered Trixie telling them that if someone who didn't believe in Halloween ate a magic sweet, then the part of Halloween it looked after would be ruined.

"What if the goblins eat the magic jellybean?" Kirsty shivered. She couldn't bear to think of Halloween without the taste of hot chocolate, or fruit gums, or toffee apples. "We have to do something, and fast!" she insisted.

"Trixie, can you make us human-size again?" Rachel asked, flying lower in the sky. "We'll have a better chance of catching the goblins on the ground."

"Of course," Trixie said. "But I won't change your wands. You might need the light!"

As soon as Kirsty and Rachel were ready, Trixie waved her wand. The girls set off at a run towards the goblins the moment their feet touched the grass. "Stop!" they yelled at the same time.

The goblins stopped eating and tried to look around, but they couldn't see through the tiny eyeholes in their white sheets.

94

"Who was that?" a goblin asked, his voice muffled by the sheet over his head.

"Who cares?" another replied. "Concentrate! We have to find that magic sweet and take it to Jack Frost."

Then a goblin peeked out from under his costume. "Oh no! It's those annoying girls again!" he yelped. "Let's get out of here!"

The goblins started to throw all of the sweets back into the baskets and bowls and bags. Then they stacked them up and tried to balance the towers of treats as they ran towards the street.

"They must have stolen sweets from almost every house!" Kirsty said, chasing a goblin with six bowls teetering in his hands.

The goblins stumbled across the playground, barely able to see. One goblin ran right up one side of a seesaw and down the other.

Another got caught on the swings. But before the girls knew it, the goblins had reached the street – and disappeared into the middle of the Halloween parade!

Moonlight's Magic

The street was full of people in costume. Kirsty watched as skeletons and witches and aliens marched by. Then, out of the corner of her eye, Kirsty glimpsed a flash of white. A ghost!

She reached out to grab the ghost's trick-or-treat bag, but then she realised the ghost wore tiny white trainers.

A goblin could never fit his huge feet into those little shoes, she thought.

Just as she had given up hope, Kirsty felt a tap on her shoulder.

"Look over there," said Rachel, pointing. Kirsty followed her friend's gaze and saw Trixie perched in a tree on the other side of the street. The fairy was waving her arms and jumping up and down. "Let's go and see what she wants – before anyone else spots her!" Rachel said, grabbing Kirsty's hand and leading her through the crowd of people.

"I'm glad you saw me," Trixie said as she flew down from the tree and landed on Rachel's shoulder. "I've spotted the goblins! They went into that park."

Rachel and Kirsty peered at the dark park nearby. "That's Windy Hollow," Rachel said with a shiver. "It won't be easy to find them in there."

"Well, let's give it our best shot," Trixie replied with a bright smile, flying into the night. The two friends slipped through the park gate and into the shadows after her.

At once, they could hear the wind that gave the park its name. It rustled through the leaves and put a chill in the air.

"It really feels like Halloween now," Kirsty whispered as she searched the inky night for signs of the goblins. There were no streetlights, and heavy clouds covered the moon. The only light came from their three fairy wands. The girls tiptoed along, stopping every few steps to try and listen for the goblins.

"Shhhh," Trixie warned them. "I think we're close." The little fairy peeked over the crest of a hill and motioned for Kirsty and Rachel to stop. "They're down there," she whispered. The girls got on their hands and knees, and crawled up the grassy slope to look over the hill.

Sure enough, the group of ghosts were

in the hollow, rooting through the stash of sweets again.

"If they have the magic jellybean, they're bound to find it soon," Rachel said, worried.

"Not if we find it first," Kirsty replied.

"Trixie, how do you feel about playing a little Halloween trick?" Kirsty's eyes brightened as she told Rachel and Trixie her plan.

"It's worth a try," Trixie said with a grin. "I can't do much while the sweet is missing, but I still have enough magic for a little trick!" She gave her wand a twirl and recited a spell:

*"The goblins think they're in disguise,
but now real ghosts are on the rise.
Raise those sheets up in the air.
Then all goblins should beware!"*

As soon as Trixie had finished speaking, the sheets that covered the goblins lifted into the air. They floated just above the goblins' heads and looked like real ghosts!

Rachel and Kirsty gave each other a thumbs-up and then spoke in their spookiest voices. "Ooooooooo," they moaned. "Give back the sweets you stole.

Ooooooooooo!"

At once, the goblins looked up and saw the sheets fluttering in the wind.

"Ghosts!" they screeched.

"Oooooooo! Give back the sweets," the girls repeated. The three friends giggled. The goblins were cowering below the ghostly sheets, shaking with fear.

Just then, a single goblin yelled, "I found the magic sweet!" He held his hand up in the air. "Hooray!"

Kirsty, Rachel and Trixie exchanged worried glances. "What do we do now?" Kirsty whispered.

"Chase him!" Rachel said. But before the friends could get to their feet, they heard a loud yowl. They saw Moonlight the mischievous kitten pounce on the goblin's back.

"Ouch!" the goblin yelped, trying to push Moonlight off.

The other goblins scattered in different directions until only the one remained. All at once, Moonlight jumped to the ground, and the last goblin darted away after his friends.

Moonlight looked up at Trixie and the two girls. *Meow*, the black kitten mewed softly. *Meow, meow, meow*, he repeated before leaping into the shadows.

"It's the magic sweet!" Trixie exclaimed. "Moonlight is telling us that the goblin dropped it!" The three friends raced down the hill to where the kitten had been.

Sure enough, there was the magic
jellybean on the ground, along with
all of the other stolen treats.

"I can't wait to get this back to
Fairyland," Trixie laughed, lifting the
sweet up in the air. As soon as she touched
it, it shrank to its original Fairyland size.
"Then there will be sweets for everyone!"

"And all of the sweets that the goblins
stole will be returned," Kirsty added.

The clouds floated away and the moon

brightened the night with a silvery light.

"We're very lucky that Moonlight came along when he did," Rachel said.

"I'm off to Fairyland," Trixie said, nodding. "Let me send you back to your street, so you can trick-or-treat!" Trixie held up her wand, and a whirl of star-shaped fairy dust circled Rachel and Kirsty. The two girls waved to Trixie. The next thing they knew, they were back on Rachel's street.

The friends looked down the street to make sure no one had seen them. Then they grinned. "No more tricks for us tonight," Kirsty said.

Rachel nodded, holding up her bag and giggling. "Now I'm ready for some sweet treats!"

The
Toffee Apple
Adventure

Contents

Ho-hum Halloween

"Trick or treat!" Rachel and Kirsty said in chorus. They had been busy collecting sweets since Trixie had gone back to Fairyland with the magic jellybean.

"We have lots of treats now," Kirsty said, looking in her bag. "I'll definitely save some chocolate for my mum. I always share my sweets with her."

Rachel laughed. "My dad loves sweets,
too. We always eat
our Halloween
sweets together,"
she smiled. Then
she looked at her
watch. "We've just
about got enough
time to go to a few
more houses before it's
time to go to the town Halloween party."

Between ringing doorbells and greeting
neighbours, Rachel and Kirsty stayed on
the lookout for Trixie. They also watched
out for Moonlight, the clever kitten. After
visiting a few more houses, Rachel pulled
out the invitation that her parents had
given her. There was a picture of a spooky
old house on the front.

"The party's at a new place," Rachel explained. "It used to be held on the other

side of town, but my parents said we'd be able to walk this year. I'm pretty sure I know where this address is."

The girls walked along the pavement. As they got closer to the party, there were more groups of children and parents going the same way. Everyone was wearing costumes. "This is it," Rachel announced, checking the address on the invitation one more time. She stared down the long path to the old Victorian house.

"Really?" Kirsty asked. "This is that spooky house we passed the other day. I thought you said no one lived here."

Overhearing the girls, a man dressed as a mad scientist stopped and raised his lab goggles. "This is the mansion where the Greens used to live," he said. "The town bought it, and they're turning it into a community centre."

"Oh, so this is where it will be," Rachel said. "My parents were part of the planning group for the centre. They must have kept the location a secret so they could surprise me!"

"Well, this is the first event they're holding here," the man replied. As he waved goodbye and walked down the curvy path, Kirsty noticed he was wearing glow-in-the-dark rubber gloves and an old lab coat.

Just then, the girls overheard a family walking up behind them. "It's too scary," a little girl said to her father, who picked her up in his arms. "I don't want to go in there," she pleaded. The girl, dressed as a koala bear, buried her head in her father's shoulder and tried not to look.

Kirsty couldn't help agreeing with the little girl. "Even the trees are creepy," she said, noticing how the bare branches made long, finger-like shadows. "It looks like a house that has a lot of secrets."

"Not you, too!" Rachel giggled. "You'll feel a lot better once we find Trixie's magic toffee apple. That will bring back the Halloween spirit." She grabbed her friend's hand and pulled her down the path towards the old mansion.

Haunted House Party

Rachel and Kirsty gasped as they walked through the front door of the mansion.

"The decorations are fantastic," Kirsty murmured.

Papier-mâché ghosts hovered in the air, and a giant spider web stretched from the floor to the ceiling. Bunches of orange and black balloons were tied to the grand staircase in the centre of the ground floor.

Next to a stone fireplace, a rock band was playing *The Monster Rock*. The musicians were all dressed as mummies, and the music filled the house. A long table of food was right next to the grand staircase. Both girls noted that there were no toffee apples to be seen.

Before the friends could take it all in, Rachel's mum rushed up to them. "I'm so glad you're here," she said. "We need people to start playing games and dancing. No one seems to be having fun."

Rachel looked about her and realised that everyone was just standing around, not talking or eating or laughing. She gave Kirsty a knowing look. No one would have any fun until the magic toffee apple was returned to Fairyland!

"We're happy to help, Mum," promised Rachel.

"OK, why don't you go to the second floor? That's where all the games are," Mrs Walker said.

Kirsty gazed up the tall staircase. It was like something out of an old movie.

"Let's start looking at the top and make  our way down," she whispered to Rachel, who nodded.

"The last magic sweet might be here."

Judging by the unhappy faces of all the party-goers, they needed to find the magic sweet fast!

When they climbed up to the second floor, the friends saw a long, narrow hallway. It was lined with bookshelves, and there were three dark wooden doors.

A sign for a different activity hung on each door. "Let's go to the pumpkin-carving room first," Rachel suggested.

As soon as they stepped inside, they heard a group of boys bickering. "Your costume is silly," one of the boys said. "We were supposed to dress up as something green."

"So what? I'm Peter Pan," the other boy said.

"Peter Pan isn't green," another retorted. "He just wears green."

Rachel and Kirsty looked at each other in surprise. "They're goblins!" they whispered, realising everyone in the group was wearing a green costume that matched his skin. One goblin was dressed as a bunch of grapes and another was a turtle. The two goblins pestering Peter Pan were dressed as trees.

All at once, a cloud of star-shaped fairy dust showered over Rachel and Kirsty. "Trixie!" they called, excited to see

their friend, who quickly ducked behind
Rachel's hair.

"Look, Trixie," said
Kirsty, pointing.
"Goblins. If they're
here, the missing
magic toffee
apple must be
nearby, too!"

"And they aren't
alone," Trixie said
softly. She motioned
to a table in the corner
where several children had started carving
pumpkins.

Rachel followed the fairy's gaze and
gasped. There, carving a pumpkin, was
Jack Frost!

Jack's Lantern

"Brrr. Just looking at him gives me
the shivers," Kirsty confessed.

There was something about Jack
Frost's magic that made the air feel icy
whenever the troublemaker was around.

"I wonder what he's up to," Rachel said.
"Let's find out."

The girls tiptoed closer and hid behind
a stand-up
skeleton. To
their surprise,
Jack Frost
was
carefully
carving
a mouth
full of
crooked
teeth
into his
pumpkin.
He leaned
back and stared
at the pumpkin
lantern. He seemed very pleased with
himself.

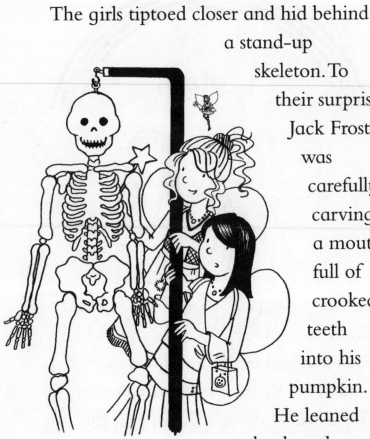

All at once, Jack Frost looked up and glared around the room. He pushed his seat back and strode over to the gang of goblins. "What's going on here?" he demanded. "I thought I told you that we can't let the humans have fun. Now hurry up and find that magic sweet!"

"Well, that explains why he's here," said Kirsty.

"He wants to make sure they find the toffee apple," Trixie said thoughtfully. "Remember, just one bite from someone who doesn't believe in Halloween, and there won't be any Halloween spirit this year."

"Then we'd better hurry up and find the apple!" Rachel said. "My parents worked so hard to get this centre ready. I don't want the first party here to be ruined!"

"What about your parents?" a voice said. The girls quickly turned around.

"Oh! Hi, Dad," Rachel gasped, brushing her hair forward to make sure Trixie was well hidden.

"I was just telling Kirsty how much fun I'm having. You all did a great job planning the party."

"Well, thanks," Mr Walker said, lifting his cowboy hat. "I wish everyone was having as much fun as you. Could you help in the next room for a minute? I need someone to run the game while I get more prizes."

"Of course," Kirsty said, hoping Rachel's dad wouldn't notice the goblins or Jack Frost.

As soon as Mr Walker left, the friends rushed to the room where a Musical Chairs sign was hanging on the door.

The girls looked around. There were about ten small children sitting on chairs in the middle of the room. They all looked bored. Most of the parents were leaning against the wall. "We'll start and stop the music," Rachel told the children, going over to the CD player.

"And take a chair away each time," Kirsty said.

"And keep an eye out for goblins!" Trixie whispered.

"OK. Is everyone ready?" Rachel called out, but only a couple of the children nodded in response. "Here goes. Find a new seat when the music stops!" Rachel instructed. Then she pushed the PLAY button.

But just as the children started to circle the empty seats, Jack Frost skipped into the room.

He was holding his pumpkin lantern, which had a giant red ribbon on it. "I won, I won," he sang, joining the children who were playing musical chairs.

Kirsty looked on, completely shocked. "I suppose I won't take a chair away," she whispered to Rachel, "since we have another player now." The best friends were used to trying to stay away from Jack Frost, but they couldn't leave when they were in charge of the game!

Rachel nodded and pushed STOP. The children all scrambled for a seat, and Jack Frost beat a child dressed as a warrior to the very last chair. He plopped his pumpkin in his lap and clapped his hands in joy. No one seemed to notice that Jack Frost was not a child. In fact, he was acting more like a child than anyone else in the room! The child dressed as a warrior dragged his feet as he went over to his father.

Just then, Rachel's dad walked through the door with a bag of puzzles and whistles and other prizes. "Thanks, girls," he said, placing the bag next to the CD player. "You can go and check out the other rooms if you want."

At first, Rachel paused. She wondered if they should stay there and keep an eye on Jack Frost. Then a loud crash came from the hallway, and she saw Moonlight the kitten skitter past the open door. A crowd of goblins raced after him!

A Hidden Kitten

"Thanks, Dad," Rachel said, giving him
a quick smile. Then she and Kirsty ran
out of the door and after the goblins.

Almost immediately, the girls skidded
to a stop. The goblins were huddled at
the top of the staircase, each looking
anxiously in a different direction.

"Where did that silly cat go?" the tallest
goblin asked.

"It just disappeared," muttered one wearing a frog costume.

"It must be magic," guessed the Peter Pan goblin.

The goblins all looked confused, but then the goblin who was dressed as a bunch of grapes stamped his foot. "The cat couldn't have disappeared!" he said. "He just ran down the stairs before we could see him. Let's split up and find him. He showed up whenever we found the other magic sweets, so he must know where the toffee apple is, too!"

Kirsty and Rachel watched as the goblins ran down the stairs and then separated to search for the missing kitten.

Trixie peeked out from behind Rachel's hair. "It's true," she whispered. "It seems like Moonlight knew where to find the other magic sweets. Maybe he can help us find the magic toffee apple."

"But first we have to find him before the goblins do," Rachel pointed out. Suddenly, Trixie raised a finger to her lips. "Did you hear that?"

Rachel and Kirsty nodded. Then they heard it again…a tiny meow.

"It sounds like it came from behind there," said Rachel, pointing to a bookshelf lining the hallway.

Kirsty examined the bookshelf on the wall. "Look!" she exclaimed. "Maybe it did!"

One book appeared to be sticking out further than the others. It was called *The Secret Staircase.* As soon as Kirsty pulled

on the book's spine, the entire bookshelf
slid to the side. There, sitting in the dark,
was Moonlight. Behind him was a spiral
staircase, almost impossible to see in the
gloom.

Meow, meow, the little cat said. He
quickly turned around and disappeared
down the mysterious staircase.

"He must want us to take this secret
passageway," Trixie said. "Oh, what fun!
Let's hurry."

Rachel and Kirsty looked at each other. It was one thing finding a hidden staircase, and another thing actually going down it. "I told you this house was full of secrets," Kirsty insisted.

"Come on!" Trixie said, flying into the dark stairwell. "How else will we save Halloween?" Trixie's wand started to glow, and the girls hurried after the fairy. The secret door slid shut behind them.

At once, the girls' wands began to glow as well. "I wonder how long it's been since someone was in here," Rachel mused, plucking a cobweb from her hair.

The wooden stairs creaked with each step she took.

"I don't know," Trixie said, "but I'm sure Moonlight has a plan."

Kirsty hoped so. She liked the idea of a secret passageway, but this one was spooky, dark and dirty, and the stairs went in such a tight circle that she was getting dizzy!

The three friends carefully descended the gloomy staircase, looking for a hint that would help them find the last magic sweet. But before they found any clues, they reached the bottom of the stairs.

"OK then," Kirsty said. "Let's find a way out."

"This looks like it might work," Rachel commented, pointing to a doorknob with a fancy flower design on it.

149

"I'll give it a try." She gave it a twist and a tug, and the door slid open slightly.

As a sliver of light entered the dark stairwell, Rachel peeked out. "It's the party room on the main floor! We're right near the food table."

Trixie and Kirsty rushed over to have a look. Trixie hovered over Rachel's head, and Kirsty ducked beneath. "Yum!" said Kirsty. "I can see popcorn, crisps, apple juice, muffins, and all kinds of sweets.

But I still don't see—"

"I see toffee apples!" Trixie declared.

"Oh!" Rachel exclaimed. "They must have just put them out. I can see them, too. And the one in the middle has a bright glittery orange wrapper!"

Just as Rachel said it, all three friends gasped.

Someone was standing by the toffee apples and rubbing his hands together gleefully. That someone was Jack Frost!

A Festive Frost

"Oh no! He mustn't eat it!" Rachel
yelled, but Kirsty stopped her from
opening the door all the way.

"We need a plan," Kirsty explained.

"She's right," Trixie agreed. "If we go
out there now, Jack Frost will spot us and
grab the toffee apple, and we won't have
a chance."

Just then, a little boy dressed as a pirate walked up to the food table, right next to Jack Frost. Jack Frost stretched his bony fingers towards the magic toffee apple.

"Shiver me timbers!" the young pirate bellowed suddenly, lifting up his eye patch for a better look. "I like your costume, matey. Did you make it yourself?"

The three friends hiding behind the door were surprised to see Jack Frost blush. "Um, well, my mother made it," he said.

Rachel and Kirsty looked at each other and giggled.

"It looks so real," the little boy said. "I want a costume like that next year."

"Well, your costume is good, too." Jack Frost muttered. Then, without even looking, he reached out and grabbed the toffee apple with the glittery wrapper.

Trixie and the girls held their breath.

"Would you like this?" he asked the boy.

Rachel thought that Jack Frost was being mean to the little pirate, but his smile looked genuine. Just as the boy was about to take the apple, a goblin ran up and snatched it from his hands. "I've got it!" the goblin shrieked.

"What? No! It was for him!" Jack Frost cried, but the goblin was in such a rush, he didn't seem to notice that Jack Frost was even there! Just then, another goblin snatched the toffee apple and held it up in the air.

"Hee, hee! Hooray for me!" the goblin hooted. "I'm going to give it to Jack Frost!" Then he ran off, holding the apple in the air.

"What's happening?" Rachel asked. "Don't they realise that Jack Frost is right here?"

"I guess not!" Trixie laughed, shaking her head.

"We have to do something!" Kirsty said.

"Let's wait and see what happens," Trixie said.

Just then, the Peter Pan goblin leaped up, clutching the toffee apple. "It's mine now!" he yelled, running across the room.

The parents at the party rolled their eyes, assuming that the goblins were children with bad manners. The Peter Pan goblin cackled with joy as he ran, but he didn't watch where he was going. He tripped over a witch's broom and went sprawling forward. The toffee apple flew from his hands and up towards the ceiling.

Suddenly, Trixie, Rachel and Kirsty spotted Moonlight, perched on the chandelier. With a swat of his paw, Moonlight batted the toffee apple towards a bunch of balloons. The apple bounced right off them! Everyone at the party was trying to ignore the horrible goblins, so no one noticed the apple whizz over their heads and through the gap in the secret door.

"Wow! You caught it!" Rachel cried, gazing at Kirsty with excitement. "This time, the magic really did come to us!"

"Good catch!" Trixie exclaimed. "Thank you so much." The Halloween Fairy beamed as she tapped the apple with her wand and it shrank back to its Fairyland size. "I guess Moonlight had a plan all along. Now I need to hurry back to Fairyland, so everyone can share in the magic of Halloween! I'll be back soon."

As Trixie disappeared in a whirl of fairy dust, Rachel and Kirsty slipped out of the secret door and joined the party.

Rachel smiled. "I can't wait until Trixie gets the last sweet back to Fairyland."

"The party feels more fun already," Kirsty said, looking around. Then her gaze caught an unusual sight. Kirsty tugged Rachel's sleeve and pointed. Jack Frost was sitting in the corner with his young pirate friend, and they were both eating toffee apples.

"Hmm. Is it possible that he wasn't after the actual magic toffee apple at all?" Kirsty wondered.

Then she and her best friend looked each other in the eye. "No," they agreed, shaking their heads and giggling.

"And he's certainly not letting the people have all the fun. He's enjoying himself as much as anyone," Rachel admitted.

"Maybe Jack Frost just didn't want to be left out of the magic of Halloween after all," suggested Kirsty.

The band started back up, and the dance floor filled with ghosts and ghouls and goblins. Rachel saw her parents laughing with a skeleton and a wizard.

Through the window, the girls noticed
a burst of glittery stars brighten the night
sky. "That must be Trixie," Kirsty said. The
best friends rushed out of the door
and found Trixie

sitting on top
of a pumpkin-
shaped bowl.

"I wanted to
come back and
thank you,"
the fairy said.
"And give you
these pumpkin
sweet jars from
the king and queen.
They are so grateful for
all of your help. Now everyone can have
a happy Halloween!"

"Thank you, Trixie. We had a lot of fun," said Rachel, lifting the lid off her sweetie jar. It was filled with jellybeans, bars of chocolate, and toffee apples – all in glittery orange wrappers. "This is very kind of you, Trixie," Kirsty added. "Thank you, and happy Halloween!"

All at once, a little black cat bounded from the shadows. As Moonlight leapt towards Trixie, he magically shrank to Fairyland size and landed in the fairy's lap.

"Oh, Moonlight!" Trixie said with a delighted smile. "Now I really am having the happiest Halloween ever!"

With that, and a final kiss to Rachel and Kirsty, the fairy and her kitten vanished in a shower of stars.

"I guess it's time to join the Halloween

party," Rachel said, smiling at her friend.

"We should celebrate," Kirsty agreed. "We've had another magical fairy adventure, and there's nothing sweeter than that!"

Now it's time for Rachel and Kirsty to help...

Ally the Dolphin Fairy

Read on for a sneak peek...

Kirsty Tate and Rachel Walker stepped
off the bus and blinked in the sunshine.
The two girls were staying with Kirsty's
gran in Leamouth for the spring holiday
and today they'd come to Lea-on-Sea,
a small seaside resort along the coast. "I've
got some shopping to do, so I'll meet you
back here at midday," Kirsty's gran said,
getting off the bus. "Have fun!"

"We will," Kirsty assured her. "See you
later, Gran." Then she turned to Rachel.
"Come on, let's go down to the beach!"

It took the girls just moments to walk
down the sandy steps to the curving bay,

which was packed with families enjoying the sun. The sky was a clear, fresh blue, and a breeze ruffled the tops of the waves. Lots of children were swimming in the sea, while shrieking seagulls soared above them, their strong white wings stretched wide.

"It's lovely," Rachel said, slipping off her shoes and wiggling her bare toes in the warm sand. She pointed to the far edge of the bay. "Let's go over there, shall we? It's a bit less crowded."

The girls made their way across the beach, zigzagging between deckchairs, windbreaks and sandcastles. Then Kirsty stopped walking suddenly and bent down. "Hey, look at this shell," she said, picking it up to show Rachel. "It's really sparkly."

Rachel peered at the fan-shaped scallop

shell, which was a creamy-white colour with pink edging. And yes – tiny golden sparkles were fizzling all over it!

Rachel's heart quickened with excitement as she looked at Kirsty. "That looks like fairy magic," she whispered.

"Just what I was thinking," Kirsty replied, smiling. "Oh! And I can feel something underneath it, too."

She flipped the shell over in her palm and both girls saw a tiny golden scroll tucked into it, tied with a pretty red ribbon. Rachel untied the ribbon and unfurled the scroll, then both girls leaned over to read the tiny writing there...

Read Ally the Dolphin Fairy to find out what adventures are in store for Kirsty and Rachel!

Christmas fun with the fairies!

Look out for the fabulous Rainbow Magic specials.
Each one features three new adventures for
Kirsty, Rachel and a special fairy friend!

www.rainbowmagicbooks.co.uk

Enjoy special days with the fairies!

Win Rainbow Magic Goodies!

There are lots of Rainbow Magic fairies, and we want to know
which one is your favourite! Send us a picture of her and tell
us in thirty words why she is your favourite and why you like
Rainbow Magic books. Each month we will put the entries into
a draw and select one winner to receive a Rainbow Magic
Sparkly T-shirt and Goody Bag!

Send your entry on a postcard to Rainbow Magic Competition,
Orchard Books, 338 Euston Road, London NW1 3BH.
Australian readers should email: childrens.books@hachette.com.au
New Zealand readers should write to Rainbow Magic Competition,
4 Whetu Place, Mairangi Bay, Auckland NZ.
Don't forget to include your name and address.
Only one entry per child.

Good luck!

Meet the fairies, play games
and get sneak peeks at
the latest books!

www.rainbowmagicbooks.co.uk

There's fairy fun for everyone on
our wonderful website.
You'll find great activities, competitions, stories and
fairy profiles, and also a special newsletter.

Get 30% off all Rainbow Magic books at
www.rainbowmagicbooks.co.uk

Enter the code RAINBOW at the checkout.
Offer ends 31 December 2013.

Offer valid in United Kingdom and Republic of Ireland only.

Meet the
Rainbow Fairies

Collect the seven original Rainbow Fairies
to find out how the adventure began!

www.rainbowmagicbooks.co.uk